My sisters
love my clothes

For Lara

B M Hn

My sisters
love my clothes

story by brendan hanrahan

pictures by lise stork

perry heights press

new york

1991

My sisters love my clothes

Published by Perry Heights Press
29 Mill River Road, Chappaqua, New York 10514
Manufactured in the United States of America.
10 9 8 7 6 5 4 3 2 1

Publisher's - Cataloging In Publication
(Prepared by Quality Books Inc.)

Hanrahan, Brendan, 1956-
　　　　My sisters love my clothes / story by brendan hanrahan, pictures by lise stork. --
　p. cm.
　SUMMARY: Louie's five sisters are always borrowing his coolest of clothes but one day, while searching for something to wear, Louie realizes that his sisters are more important than cool clothes.
　ISBN 0-9630181-0-8

　1. Clothing and dress -- Fiction.   2. Brothers and sisters -- Fiction.
　I. Stork, Lise.   II. Title.

PZ7　　　　　　　　　　　　　　[E]

To Terence Balagia--whose sisters, Sarah and Rebecca, love *him*.

I have this problem. You see, I have five sisters.
That's not the problem though--the problem is they all
love to wear my clothes.

I do have some pretty cool clothes, and I understand
why they like them. My problem starts when I want
to get dressed but can't find anything to wear, which
happened today.

When my warm feet hit the cold floor in the morning, the first thing I look for is a nice pair of warm, thick socks.

This morning I want my extra high, three green stripe, tube socks. My friend Nels got them for me from his brother who goes to high school.

The problem is my socks are nowhere to be found.

While my feet are freezing, I yell down the hall, "Where are my three green stripe, tube socks?"

My sister Nora sticks her head out of the bathroom and says, "Oh Louie, your socks are perfect for my soccer tryouts. Can I p-l-e-a-s-e wear them? I promise to wash them!"

I really want to wear those socks-- but I'm basically a good brother, and Nora's not so bad, and they do need washing.

Anyway, I could wear my primo Hawaiian surfing jams that my dad brought back from Hawaii instead. They are from a real surf shop where real surfers shop. With my surfing jams, you don't need three green stripe tube socks.

Of course, there aren't any jams in my drawers either. "Who's got my jams?" I yell again.

My sister Ella yells back, "Oh Louie, your jams are perfect for the mall, and I'm meeting all my friends there. Can I give them back to you tonight...that's all, just until tonight!"

"Just until tonight," I think to myself. Well--Ella's not so bad, and she does let me stay up late and watch TV when she babysits. Besides, maybe plain old jeans would be better in case Nels wants to play slow motion football.

I suppose I could wear my shark bite T-shirt. It has a hole that looks like a great white shark took a big bite out of it with rips where his teeth got stuck and red paint all around the edges that looks like blood.

When kids see it, they go wild.

For a minute, I think it must be in the laundry because it isn't in my drawers. But then I'm yelling down the hall again, "Where's my shark bite T-shirt!"

My sister Sarah says, "Oh Louie, I'm going to a party, and your shark bite T-shirt will be the rage. If you let me borrow it, I'll give you and Nels a ride to the movies!"

"H-m-m-m," I think. I know Nels
wants to see that new alien movie
with all the slime.

Besides, when I wear my shark shirt my friends go wild. They jump on me and yell "Shark Attack!" It might be safer to wear some other plain, old T-shirt.

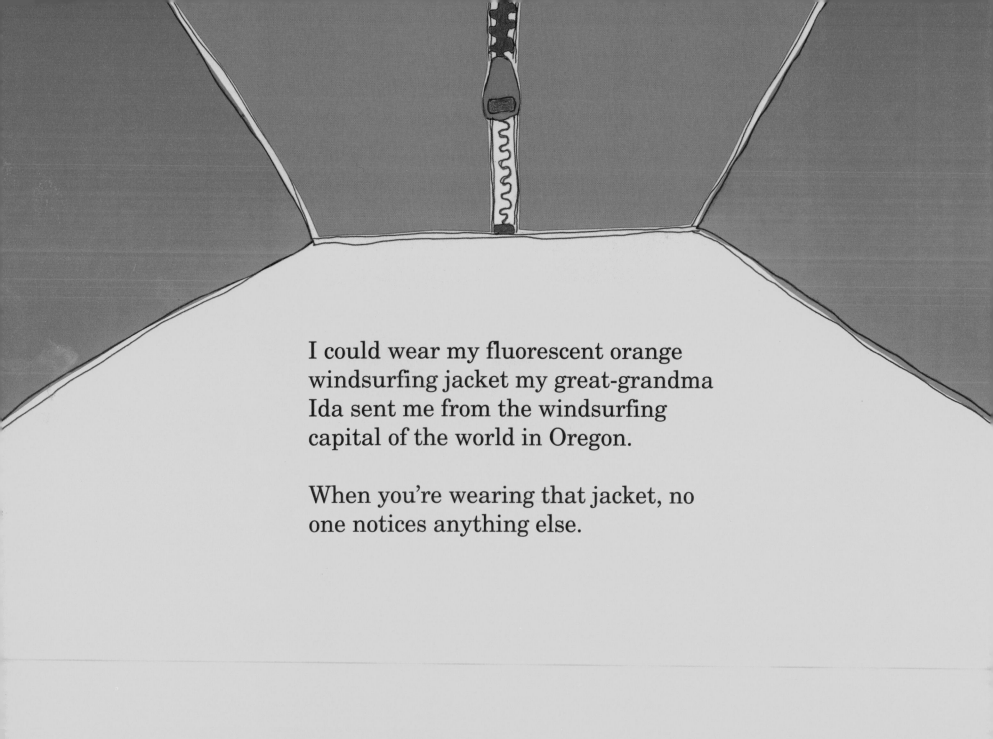

I could wear my fluorescent orange windsurfing jacket my great-grandma Ida sent me from the windsurfing capital of the world in Oregon.

When you're wearing that jacket, no one notices anything else.

By now, I'm not surprised it's not in my closet. Once again I'm yelling, "Where's my fluorescent orange windsurfing jacket?"

I'm not even surprised when my oldest sister, Heather, says, "Oh Louie, I've got to have a wild jacket like this to go sailing this weekend. If I can borrow it, I'll take you to a football game at my school!"

I don't get to do too much with Heather anymore and I love football games. It would be worth it to wear a plain, old jacket if I got to go to a game with her.

Then I remember my favorite duckbilled fishing cap.
Not many people have ever seen a duckbilled fishing
cap. It's very unusual and has a big, long brim, like a
duck's bill.

It makes me feel special, no matter what I'm wearing.

Like everything else, I can't find my duckbilled hat anywhere. I'm just about to yell again when my littlest sister, Rachel, wanders down the hall with nothing on but my duckbilled cap and her diapers.

I could just grab it, but I know she would scream her lungs out. She may be little, but she can scream like a siren on a firetruck. Even my duckbilled cap isn't worth that.

Along with all the other plain, old clothes I'm wearing today, I might as well wear my plain, old baseball cap.

The problem is I always end up wearing plain, old, boring clothes: plain socks, old jeans, boring T-shirt, plain old jacket and a regular, old baseball cap.

I'm plain old me--the kid who should be wearing the most outrageous clothes you've ever seen.

The kid whose sisters are wearing the most outrageous clothes you've ever seen.

On the other hand, plain, old me has five, very cool sisters.

So what if they are wearing my clothes today?

Tomorrow my three green stripe socks will be fresh and clean because Nora will have washed them.

I'll wear my jams and stay up late to watch TV when Ella babysits.

I can wear my shark bite T-shirt to the alien movie that Sarah is taking me and Nels to see.

I can wear my fluorescent orange windsurfing jacket when I go to the football game with Heather.

And I don't have to listen to Rachel cry.

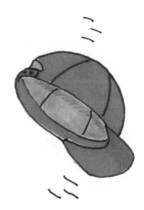

Maybe I don't have a problem after all.

Book design by Brendan Hanrahan & Lise Stork
Endpaper design by Lise Stork
Edited by Melanie Lewis
Executive Publisher - Nancy Hanrahan
Manufactured by Berryville Graphics - KidPrint